THE ULTIMATE EARTH

a novella by

JACK WILLIAMSON

PHOENIX PICK BOOKLETS

an imprint of

Rockville, Maryland

Originally published in *Analog Science Fiction & Fact*, December 2000.

This is a work of fiction. Any resemblance to any actual persons, events or localities is purely coincidental and beyond the intent of the author and publisher.

ISBN: 978-1-61242-154-4

www.PhoenixPick.com
Great Science Fiction at Great Prices

Published by Phoenix Pick
an imprint of Arc Manor
P. O. Box 10339
Rockville, MD 20849-0339
www.ArcManor.com

1

WE LOVED UNCLE PEN. The name he gave us was too hard for us to say, and we made it Sandor Pen. As early as we could understand, the robots had told us that we were clones, created to watch the skies for danger and rescue Earth from any harm. They had kept us busy with our lessons and our chores and our workouts in the big centrifuge, but life in our little burrow left us little else to do. His visits were our best excitement.

He never told us when he was coming. We used to watch for him, looking from the high dome on the Tycho rim, down across the field of Moondust the digging machines had leveled. Standing huge on the edge of it, they were metal monsters out of space, casting long black shadows across the gray waste of rocks and dust and crater pits.

His visit on our seventh birthday was a wonderful surprise. Tanya saw him landing and called us up to the dome. His ship was a bright teardrop, shining in the black shadow of a gigantic metal insect. He jumped out of it in a sleek silvery suit that fitted like his skin. We waited inside the air lock to watch him peel it off. He was a small lean man, who looked graceful as a girl but still very strong. Even his body was exciting to see, though Dian ran and hid because he looked so strange.

Naked, his body had a light tan that darkened in the sunlit dome and faded fast when he went below. His face was a narrow heart-shape, his golden eyes enormous. Instead of hair like ours, his head was capped with sleek, red-brown fur. He needed no clothing, he told us, because his sex organs were internal.

He called Dian when he missed her, and she crept back to share the gifts he had brought from Earth. There were sweet fruits we had never tasted, strange toys, stranger games that he had to show us how to play. For Tanya and Dian there were dolls that sang strange songs in voices we couldn't understand and played loud music on tiny instruments we had never heard.

The best part was just the visit with him in the dome. Pepe and Casey had eager questions about life on the new Earth. Were there cities? Wild animals? Alien creatures? Did people live in houses, or underground in tunnels like ours? What did he do for a living? Did he have a wife? Children like us?

He wouldn't tell us much. Earth, he said, had changed since our parents knew it. It was now so different that he wouldn't know where to begin, but he let us take turns looking at it through the big telescope. Later, he promised, if he could find space gear to fit us, he would take us up to orbit the Moon and loop toward it for a closer look. Now, however, he was working to learn all he could about the old Earth, the way it had been ages ago, before the great impacts.

He showed it to us in the holo tanks and the brittle old paper books, the way it was with white ice caps over the poles and bare brown deserts on the continents. Terraformed, the new Earth had no deserts and no ice. Under the bright cloud spirals, the land was green where the sun struck it, all the way over the poles. It looked so wonderful that Casey and Pepe begged him to take us back with him to let us see it for ourselves.

"I'm sorry." He shook his neat, fur-crowned head. "Terribly sorry, but you can't even think of a trip to Earth."

We were looking from the dome. Earth stood high in the black north, where it always stood. Low in the west, the slow Sun blazed hot on the new mountains the machines had piled up around the spaceport, and filled the craters with ink.

Dian had learned by now to trust him. She sat on his knee, gazing up in adoration at his quirky face. Tanya stood behind him, playing a little game. She held her hand against his back to bleach the golden tan, and took it away to watch the Sun erase the print.

Looking hurt, Casey asked why we couldn't think of a trip to Earth.

"You aren't like me." That was very true. Casey has a wide black face with narrow Chinese eyes and straight black hair. "And you belong right here."

"I don't look like anybody." Casey shrugged. "Or belong to you."

"Of course you don't." Uncle Pen was gently patient. "But you do belong to the station and your great mission." He looked at me. "Remind him, Dunk."

My clone father was Duncan Yarrow. The master computer that runs the station often spoke with his holo voice. He had told us how we had been cloned again and again from the tissue cells left frozen in the cryostat.

"Sir, that's true." I felt a little afraid of Uncle Pen, but proud of all the station had done. "My holo father has told us how the big impacts killed

Earth and killed it again. We have always brought it back to life." My throat felt dry. I had to gulp, but I went on. "If Earth's alive now, that's because of us."

"True. Very true." He nodded, with an odd little smile. "But perhaps you don't know that your little Moon has suffered a heavy impact of his own. If you are alive today, you owe your lives to me."

"To you?" We all stared at him, but Casey was nodding. "To you and the digging machines? I've watched them and wondered what they were digging for. When did that object hit the Moon?"

"*¿Quién sabe?*" He shrugged at Pepe, imitating the gesture and the voice Pepe had learned from his holo father. "It was long ago. Perhaps a hundred thousand years, perhaps a million. I haven't found a clue."

"The object?" Pepe frowned. "Something hit the station?"

"A narrow miss." Uncle Pen nodded at the great dark pit in the crater rim just west of us. "The ejecta smashed the dome and buried everything. The station was lost and almost forgotten. Only a myth till I happened on it."

"The diggers?" Casey turned to stare down at the landing field where Uncle Pen had left his flyer in the shadows of those great machines and the mountains they had built. "How did you know where to dig?"

"The power plant was still running," Uncle Pen said. "Keeping the computer alive. I was able to detect its metal shielding and then its radiation."

"We thank you." Pepe came gravely to shake his hand. "I'm glad to be alive."

"So am I," Casey said. "If I can get to Earth." He saw Uncle Pen beginning to shake his head, and went on quickly, "Tell us what you know about the Earth impacts and how we came down to terraform the Earth and terraform it again when it was killed again."

"I don't know what you did."

"You have showed us the difference we made," Casey said. "The land is all green now, with no deserts or ice."

"Certainly it has been transformed." Nodding, Uncle Pen stopped to smile at Tanya as she left her game with the Sun on his back and came to sit cross-legged at his feet. "Whatever you did was ages ago. Our historians are convinced that we've done more ourselves."

"You changed the Earth?" Casey was disappointed and a little doubtful. "How?"

"We removed undersea ledges and widened straits to reroute the ocean circulation and warm the poles. We diverted rivers to fill new lakes and bring rain to deserts. We engineered new life-forms that improved the whole biocosm."

"But still you owe us something. We put you there."

"Of course." Uncle Pen shrugged. "Excavating the station, I uncovered evidence that the last impact annihilated life on Earth. The planet had been reseeded sometime before the lunar impact occurred."

"We did it." Casey grinned. "You're lucky we were here."

"Your ship?" Pepe had gone to stand at the edge of the dome, looking down at the monster machines and Uncle Pen's neat little flyer, so different from the rocket spaceplanes we had seen in the old video holos. "Can it go to other planets?"

"It can." He nodded. "The planets of other suns."

Tanya's eyes went wide, and Pepe asked, "How does it fly in space with no rocket engines?"

"It doesn't," he said. "It's called a slider. It slides around space, not through it."

"To the stars?" Tanya whispered. "You've been to other stars?"

"To the planets of other stars." He nodded gravely. "I hope to go again when my work here is finished."

"Across the light-years?" Casey was awed. "How long does it take?"

"No time at all." He smiled at our wonderment. "Not in slider flight. Outside of space-time, there is no time. But there are laws of nature, and time plays tricks that may surprise you. I could fly across a hundred light-years to another star in an instant of my own time and come back in another instant, but two hundred years would pass here on Earth while I was away."

"I didn't know." Tanya's eyes went wider still. "Your friends would all be dead."

"We don't die."

She shrank away as if suddenly afraid of him. Pepe opened his mouth to ask something, and shut it without a word.

He chucked at our startlement. "We've engineered ourselves, you see, more than we've engineered the Earth."

Casey turned to look out across the shadowed craters at the huge globe of Earth, the green Americas blazing on the sunlit face, Europe and Africa only a shadow against the dark. He stood there a long time and came slowly back to stand in front of Uncle Pen.

"I'm going down to see the new Earth when I grow up." His face set stubbornly. "No matter what you say."

"Are you growing wings?" Uncle Pen laughed and reached a golden arm to pat him on the head. "If you didn't know, the impact smashed all your old rocket craft to junk."

He drew quickly back.

"Really, my boy, you do belong here." Seeing his hurt, Uncle Pen spoke more gently. "You were cloned for your work here at the station. A job that ought to make you proud."

Casey made an angry swipe across his eyes with the back of his hand and swallowed hard, but he kept his voice even.

"Maybe so. But where's any danger now?"

Uncle Pen had an odd look. He took a long moment to answer.

"We are not aware of any actual threat from another impacting bolide. All the asteroids that used to approach Earth's orbit have been diverted, most of them steered into the Sun."

"So?" Casey's dark chin had a defiant jut. "Why did you want to dig us up?"

"For history." Uncle Pen looked away from us, up at the huge, far-off Earth. "I hope you try to understand what that means. The resurfaced Earth had lost nearly every trace of our beginning. Historians were trying to prove that we had evolved on some other planet and migrated here. Tycho Station is proof that Earth is the actual mother world. I've found our roots here under the rubble."

"I guess you can be proud of that," Casey said, "but who needs the station now?"

"Nobody, really." He shrugged, with an odd little twist of his golden lips, and I thought he felt sorry for Casey. "If another disaster did strike the Earth, which isn't likely at all, it could be repeopled by the colonies."

"So you dug us up for nothing?"

"If you knew what I have done," Pen leaned and reached as if to hug him, but he shrank farther away. "It wasn't easy! We've had to invent and improvise. We had to test the tissue cells still preserved in the cryostat, and build new equipment in the maternity lab. A complex system. It had to be tested." He smiled down into Tanya's beaming devotion. "The tests have turned out well."

"So we are just an experiment?"

"Aren't you glad to be alive?"

"Maybe," Casey muttered bitterly. "If I can get off the Moon. I don't want to sit here till I die, waiting for nothing at all."

Looking uncomfortable, Pen just reached down to lift Tanya up in his arms.

"We were meant for more than that," Casey told him. "I want a life."

"Please, my dear boy, you must try to understand." Patiently, Uncle Pen shook his furry head. "The station is a precious historic monument, our sole surviving relic of the early Earth and early man. You are part of it. I'm sorry if you take that for a misfortune, but there is certainly no place for you on Earth."

2

SANDOR PEN KEPT COMING to the Moon as we grew up, though not so often. He brought tantalizing gifts. Exotic fruits that had to be eaten before they spoiled. New games and difficult puzzles. Little holo cubes that had held living pictures of us, caught us year after year as we grew up from babies in the maternity lab. He was always genial and kind, though I thought he came to care less for us as we grew older.

His main concern was clearly the station itself. He cleared junk and debris out of the deepest tunnels, which had been used for workshops and storage, and stocked them again with new tools and spare parts that the robots could use to repair themselves and maintain the station.

Most of his time on the visits was spent in the library and museum with Dian and her holo mother. He studied the old books and holos and paintings and sculptures, carried them away to be restored, and brought identical copies back to replace them. For a time he had the digging machines busy again, removing rubble from around the station and grinding it up to make concrete for a massive new retaining wall that they poured to reinforce the station foundation.

For our twenty-first birthday, he had the robots measure us for space suits like his own. Sleek and mirror-bright, they fitted like our skins and let us feel at home outside the dome. We wore them down to see one of our old rocket spaceplanes, standing on the field beside his little slipship. His robots had dug it out of a smashed hangar, and he now had them rebuilding it with new parts from Earth.

One of the great digging machines had extended a leverlike arm to hold it upright. A robot was replacing a broken landing strut, fusing it smoothly in place with some process that made no glow of heat. Casey spoke to the robot, but it ignored him. He climbed up to knock on the door. It responded with a brittle computer voice that was only a rattle in our helmets.

"Open up," he told it. "Let us in."

"Admission denied." Its hard machine voice had Pen's accent.

"By what authority?"

"By the authority of Director Sandor Pen, Lunar Research Site."

"Ask the director to let us in."

"Admission denied."

"So you think." Casey shook his head, his words a sardonic whisper in my helmet. "If you know how to think."

Back inside the air lock, Pen had waited to help us shuck off the mirror suits. Casey thanked him for the gift and asked if the old spaceplane would be left here on the Moon.

"Forget what you're thinking." He gave Casey a penetrating glance. "We're taking it down to Earth."

"I wish I could come."

"I'm sorry you can't." His face was firmly set, but a flush of pleasure turned it a richer gold. "It's to stand at the center of our new historic memorial, located on the Australian subcontinent. It presents our reconstruction of the prehistoric past. The whole story of the pre-impact planet and pre-impact man."

He paused to smile at Tanya. Flushed pink, she smiled back at him.

"It's really magnificent! Finding the lunar site was my great good fortune, and working it has been my life for many years. It has filled a gap in human history. Answered questions that scholars had fought over for ages. You yourselves have a place there, with a holographic diorama of your childhood."

Casey asked again why we couldn't see it. "Because you belong here." Impatience edged his voice. "And because of the charter that allowed us to work the site. We agreed to restore the station to its original state, and to import no genetic materials from it that might contaminate the Earth. We are to leave the site exactly as it was before the impact, protected and secured from any future trespass."

We all felt sick with loss on the day he told us his work at the site was done. As a farewell gift, he took us two by two to orbit the Moon. Casey and I went up together, sitting behind him in his tiny slipship. We had seen space and Earth from the dome all our lives, but the flight was still an exciting adventure.

The mirror hull was invisible from inside, so that our seats seemed to float free in open space. The Moon's gray desolation spread wider beneath us, and dwindled again to a bright bubble floating in a gulf of darkness. Though Pen touched nothing I saw, the stars blazed suddenly brighter, the Milky Way a broad belt of gem-strewn splendor all around us. The Sun was dimmed and hugely magnified to let us see the dark spots across its face.

Still he touched nothing and I felt no new motion, but now Australia expanded. The deserts were gone. A long new sea lay across the center of the continent, crescent-shaped and vividly blue.

"The memorial." He pointed to a broad tongue of green land thrust into the crescent. "If you ever get to Earth—which I don't expect—you could meet your doubles there in the Tycho exhibit."

Casey asked, "Is Mona there?"

Mona Lisa Live was the professional name of the woman Casey's father brought with him when he forced his way aboard the escape plane just ahead of the first impact. We knew them only from their holo images, he with the name "El Chino" and the crossed flags of Mexico and China tattooed across his black chest, she with the Leonardo painting on her belly.

Those ancient images had been enough to let us all catch the daring spirit and desperate devotion that had brought them finally to the Moon from the Medellin nightclub where he found her. From his first glimpse of her holo, Casey had loved her and dreamed of a day when they might be together again. I'd heard him ask my holo father why she had not been cloned with us.

"Ask the computer." He shrugged in the fatalistic way he had when his voice had its dry computer undertone. "It could have been done. Her tissue specimens are still preserved in the cryostat."

"Do you know why she wasn't cloned?"

"The computer seldom explains." He shrugged again. "If you want my own guess, she and Kell reached the Moon as unexpected intruders. The maternity lab was not prepared to care for them or their clones."

"Intruders?" Casey's dark face turned darker. "At least DeFort thought their genes were worth preserving. If I'm worth cloning, Mona ought to be. Someday she will be."

Back in the station dome, Pen made his final farewell. We thanked him for that exciting glimpse of the far-off Earth, for the space suits and all his gifts, for restoring us to life. A trifling repayment, he said, for all he had found at the station. He shook our hands, kissed Tanya and Dian, and got into his silvery suit. We followed him down to the air lock. Tanya must have loved him more than I knew. She broke into tears and ran off to her room as the rest of us watched his bright little teardrop float away toward Earth.

"We put them down there," Casey muttered. "We have a right to see what we have done."

When the robots left the restored spaceplane standing on its own landing gear, the digging machine crept away to join the others. Busy again, they were digging a row of deep pits. We watched them bury themselves under the rubble, leaving only a row of new craters that might become a puzzle, I thought, to later astronomers. Casey called us back to the dome to watch a tank truck crawling out of the underground hangar dug into the crater rim.

"We're off to Earth!" He slid his arm around Pepe. "Who's with us?"

Arne scowled at him. "Didn't you hear Sandor?"

"Sandor's gone." He grinned at Pepe. "We have a plan of our own."

They hadn't talked about it, but I had heard their whispers and seen them busy in the shops. Though the spacebending science of the slipship was still a mystery to us, I knew the robots had taught them astronautics and electronics. I knew they had made holos of Pen, begging him to say more about the new Earth than he ever would.

"I don't know your plan." Arne made a guttural grunt. "But I have seen the reports of people who went down to evaluate our terraforming. They've never found anything they liked, and never got back to the Moon."

"¿Qué importa?" Pepe shrugged. "Better that than wasting our lives waiting por nada."

"We belong here." Stubbornly, Arne echoed what Pen had said. "Our mission is just to keep the station alive. Certainly not to throw ourselves away on insane adventures. I'm staying here."

Dian chose to stay with him, though I don't think they were in love. Her love was the station itself, with all its relics of the old Earth. Even as a little child, she had always wanted to work with her holo mother, recording everything that Pen took away to be copied and returned.

Tanya had set her heart on Sandor Pen. I think she had always dreamed that someday he would take her with him back to Earth. She was desolate and bitter when he left without her, her pride in herself deeply hurt.

"He did love us when we were little," she sobbed when Pepe begged her to join him and Casey. "But just because we were children. Or just interesting pets. Interesting because we aren't his kind of human, and people that live forever don't have children."

Pepe begged again, I think because he loved her. Whatever they found on Earth, it would be bigger than our tunnels, and surely more exciting. She cried and kissed him and chose to stay. The new Earth had no place for her. Sandor wouldn't want her, even if she found him. She promised to listen for their radio and pray they came back safe.

I had always been the station historian. Earth was where history was happening. I shook hands with Pepe and Casey and agreed to go with them.

"You won't belong," Tanya warned us. "You'll have to look out for yourselves."

She found water canteens and ration packs for us, and reminded us to pack safari garments to wear when we got out of our space gear. We took turns in the dome, watching the tank truck till it reached the plane and the robots began pumping fuel.

"Time." Casey wore a grin of eager expectation. "Time to say good-bye."

Dian and Arne shook our hands, wearing very solemn faces. Tanya clung a long time to Pepe and kissed me and Casey, her face so tearstained and drawn that I ached with pity for her. We got into our shining suits, went out to the plane, climbed the landing stair. Again the door refused to open.

Casey stepped back to speak on his helmet radio.

"Priority message from Director Sandor Pen." His crackling voice was almost Pen's. "Special orders for restored spaceplane SP2469."

The door responded with a clatter of speech that was alien to me.

"Orders effective now," Casey snapped. "Tycho Station personnel K.C. Kell, Pedro Navarro, and Duncan Yare are authorized to board for immediate passage to Earth."

Silently, the door swung open.

I had expected to find a robot at the controls, but we found ourselves alone in the nose cone, the pilot seat empty. Awed by whatever the plane had become, we watched it operate itself. The door swung shut. Air seals hissed. The engines snorted and roared. The ship trembled, and we lifted off the Moon.

Looking back for the station, all I found was the dome, a bright little eye peering into space from the rugged gray peaks of the crater rim. It shrank till I lost it in the great lake of black shadow and the bright black peak at the center of the Tycho crater. The Moon dwindled till we saw it whole, gray and impact-battered, dropping behind us into a black and bottomless pit.

Pen's flight in the slipship may have taken an hour or an instant. In the old rocket ship, we had time to watch three full rotations of the slowly swelling planet ahead. The jets were silent through most of the flight, with only an occasional whisper to correct our course. We floated in free fall, careful not to blunder against the controls. Taking turns belted in the seats, we tried to sleep but seldom did. Most of the time we spent searching Earth with binoculars, searching for signs of civilization.

"Nothing," Casey muttered again and again. "Nothing that looks like a city, a railway, a canal, a dam. Nothing but green. Only forest, jungle, grassland. Have they let the planet return to nature?"

"*Tal vez.*" Pepe always shrugged. "*Pero o no.* We are still too high to tell."

At last the jets came back to life, steering us down into air-breaking orbit. Twice around the puzzling planet, and Australia exploded ahead. The jets thundered. We fell again, toward the wide tongue of green land between the narrow cusps of that long crescent lake.

3

LOOKING FROM THE WINDOWS, we found the spaceplane standing on an elevated pad at the center of a long quadrangle covered with tended lawns, shrubs and banks of brilliant flowers. Wide avenues all around it were walled with buildings that awed and amazed me.

"Sandor's Tycho Memorial!" Pepe jogged my ribs. "There's the old monument at the American capital! I know it from Dian's videos."

"Ancient history." Casey shrugged as if it hardly mattered. "I want to see Earth today."

Pepe opened the door. In our safari suits, we went out on the landing for a better view. The door shut. I heard it hiss behind us, sealing itself. He turned to stare again. The monument stood at the end of the quadrangle, towering above its image in a long reflecting pool, flanked on one side by a Stonehenge in gleaming silver, on the other by a sandbanked Sphinx with the nose restored.

We stood goggling at the old American capital at the other end of the mall, the British Houses of Parliament to its right, and Big Ben tolling the time. The Kremlin adjoined them, gilded onion domes gleaming above the grim redbrick walls. The Parthenon, roofed and new and magnificent as ever, stood beyond them on a rocky hill.

Across the quadrangle I found the splendid domes of the Taj Mahal, Saint Peter's Basilica, the Hagia Sophia from ancient Istanbul. On higher ground in the distance, I recognized the Chrysler Building from old New York, the Eiffel Tower from Paris, a Chinese pagoda, the Great Pyramid clad once again in smooth white marble. Farther off, I found a gray mountain ridge that copied the familiar curve of Tycho's rim, topped with the shine of our own native dome.

"We got here!" Elated, Pepe slapped Casey's back. "Now what?"

"They owe us." Casey turned to look again. "We put them here, whenever it was. This ought to remind them how they got here and what we've given them."

"If they care." Pepe turned back to the door. "Let's see if we can call Sandor."

"Facility closed." We heard the door's toneless robot voice. "Admission denied by order of Tycho Authority."

"Let us in!" Casey shouted. "We want the stuff we left aboard. Clothing, backpacks, canteens. Open the door so we can get them."

"Admission denied."

He hit the door with his fist and kissed his bruised knuckles.

"Admission denied."

"We're here, anyhow."

Pepe shrugged and started down the landing stair. A strange bellow stopped him, rolling back from the walls around. It took us a moment to see that it came from a locomotive chuffing slowly past the Washington Monument, puffing white steam. Hauling a train of open cars filled with seated passengers, it crept around the quadrangle, stopping often to let riders off and on.

The Sun was high, and we shaded our eyes to study them. All as lean and trim as Sandor, and often nude, they had the same nut-brown skins. Many carried bags or backpacks. A few scattered across the lawns and gardens, most waited at the corners for signal lights to let them cross the avenue.

"Tourists, maybe?" I guessed. "Here to see Sandor's recovered history?"

"But I see no children." Casey shook his head. "You'd think they'd bring the children."

"They're people, anyhow." Pepe grinned hopefully. "We'll find somebody to tell us more than Sandor did."

We climbed down the stairs, on down a wide flight of steps to a walk that curved through banks of strange and fragrant blooms. Ahead of us a couple had stopped. The woman looked a little odd, I thought, with her head of short ginger-hued fur instead of hair, yet as lovely as Mona had looked in the holos made when she and El Chino reached the Moon.

The man was youthful and handsome as Sandor. I thought they were in love.

Laughing at something he had said, she ran a little way ahead and turned to pose for his camera, framed between the monument and the Sphinx. She had worn a scarlet shawl around her shoulders. At a word from him, she whipped it off and smiled for his lens. Her daintily nippled breasts had been pale beneath the shawl, and he waited for the sun to color them.

We watched till he had snapped the camera. Laughing again, she ran back to toss the shawl around his shoulders and throw her arms around him. They clung together for a long kiss. We had stopped a dozen yards away. Casey spoke hopefully when they turned to face us.

"Hello?"

They stared blankly at us. Casey managed an uncertain smile, but a nervous sweat had filmed his dark Oriental face.

"Forgive us, please. Do you speak English? *Français? ¿Español?*"

They frowned at him, and the man answered with a stream of vowels that were almost music and a rattle of consonants I knew I could never learn to imitate. I caught a hint of Sandor's odd accent but nothing like our English. They moved closer. The man pulled the little camera out of his bag, clicked it at Casey, stepped nearer to get his head. Laughing at him, the woman came to pose again beside Casey, slipping a golden arm around him for a final shot.

"We came in that machine. Down from the Moon!" Desperation on his face, he gestured at the spaceplane behind us, turned to point toward the Moon's pale disk in the sky above the Parthenon, waved to show our flight from it to the pedestal. "We've just landed from Tycho Station. If you understand—"

Laughing at him, they caught hands and ran on toward the Sphinx.

"What the hell!" Staring after them, he shook his head. "What the bloody hell!"

"They don't know we're real." Pepe chuckled bitterly. "They take us for dummies. Part of the show."

We followed a path that led toward the Parthenon and stopped at the curb to watch the traffic flowing around the quadrangle. Cars, buses, vans, occasional trucks; they reminded me of street scenes in pre-impact videos. A Yellow Cab pulled up beside us. A woman sprang out. Slim and golden-skinned, she was almost a twin of the tourist who had posed with Casey.

The driver, however, might have been an unlikely survivor from the old Earth. Heavy, swarthy, wheezing for his breath, he wore dark glasses and a grimy leather jacket. Lighting a cigarette, he hauled himself out of the cab, waddled around to open the trunk, handed the woman a folded tripod, and grunted sullenly when she tipped him.

Casey walked up to him as he was climbing back into the cab.

"Sir!" He seemed not to hear, and Casey called louder. "Sir!"

Ignoring us, he got into the cab and pulled away. Casey turned with a baffled frown to Pepe and me.

"Did you see his face? It was dead! Some stiff plastic. His eyes are blind, behind those glasses. He's some kind of robot, no more alive than our robots on the Moon."

Keeping a cautious distance, we followed the woman with the tripod. Ignoring us, she stopped to set it up to support a flat round plate of some black stuff. As she stepped away, a big transparent bubble swelled out of the plate, clouded, turned to silver. She leaned to peer into it.

Venturing closer, I saw that the bubble had become a circular window that framed the Washington Monument, the Statue of Liberty, and the Sphinx. They seemed oddly changed, magnified and brighter, suddenly in motion. Everything shook. The monument leaned and toppled, crushing the statue. The Sphinx looked down across the fragments, intact and forever enigmatic.

I must have come too close. The woman turned with an irritated frown to brush me away as if I had been an annoying fly. Retreating, I looked again. As she bent again to the window, the sky in it changed. The Sun exploded into a huge, dull-red ball that turned the whole scene pink. Close beside it was a tiny, bright-blue star. Our spaceplane took shape in the foreground, the motors firing and white flame washing the pedestal, as if it were taking off to escape catastrophe.

Awed into silence, Casey gestured us away.

"An artist!" Pepe whispered. "An artist at work."

We walked on past the Parthenon and waited at the corner to cross the avenue. Pepe nodded at the blue-clad cop standing out on the pavement with a whistle and a white baton, directing traffic. "Watch him. He's mechanical."

So were most of the drivers. The passengers, however, riding in the taxis and buses or arriving on the train, looked entirely human, as live as Sandor himself, eager as the tourists of the pre-impact Earth to see these monumental restorations of their forgotten past.

They flocked the sidewalks, climbed the Capital steps to photograph the quadrangle and one another, wandered around the corner and on down the avenue. We fell in with them. They seldom noticed Pepe or me, but sometimes stopped to stare at Casey or take his picture.

"One more robot!" he muttered. "That's what they take me for."

We spent the rest of the day wandering replicated streets, passing banks, broker's offices, shops, bars, hairdressers, restaurants, police stations. A robot driver had parked his van in front of a bookstore to unload cartons stamped *Encyclopaedia Britannica*. A robot beggar was rattling coins in a tin cup. A robot cop was pounding in pursuit of a red-spattered robot fugitive. We saw slim gold-skinned people, gracefully alive, entering restaurants and bars, trooping into shops, emerging with their purchases.

Footsore and hungry before the day was over, we followed a tantalizing aroma that led us to a line of golden folk waiting under a sign that read:

STEAK PLUS!
PRIME ANGUS BEEF
DONE TO YOUR ORDER

Pepe fretted that we had no money for a meal.

"We'll eat before we tell them," Casey said.

"They're human, anyhow." Pepe grasped for some crumb of comfort. "They like food."

"I hope they're human."

Standing in line, I watched and listened to those ahead of us, hoping for any link of human contact, finding none at all. A few turned to give us puzzled glances. One man stared at Casey till I saw his fists clenching. Their speech sometimes had rhythm and pitch that made an eerie music, but I never caught a hint of anything familiar.

A robot at the door was admitting people a few at a time. His bright-lensed eyes looked behind us when we reached him. Finding nobody, he shut the door.

Limping under Earth gravity, growing hungrier and thirstier, we drifted on until the avenue ended at a high wall of something clear as glass, which cut the memorial off like a slicing blade. Beyond the wall lay an open landscape that recalled Dian's travel videos of tropical Africa. A line of trees marked a watercourse that wound down a shallow valley.

Zebras and antelope grazed near us, unalarmed by a dark-maned lion watching sleepily from a little hill.

"There's water we could drink." Pepe nodded at the stream. "If we can get past the wall."

We walked on till it stopped us. Seamless, hard and slick, too tall for us to climb, it ran on in both directions as far as we could see. Too tired to go farther, we sat there on the curb watching the freedom of the creatures beyond till dusk and a chill in the air drove us back to look for shelter. What we found was a stack of empty cartons behind a discount furniture outlet. We flattened a few of them to make a bed, ripped up the largest to cover us, and tried to sleep.

"You can't blame Sandor," Pepe muttered as we lay there shivering under our cardboard. "He told us we'd never belong."

4

WE DOZED ON OUR CARDBOARD pallet, aching under the heavy drag of Earth's gravity through a never-ending night, and woke stiff and cold and desperate. I almost wished we were back on the Moon.

"There has to be a hole in the fence," Casey tried to cheer us. "To let the tourists in."

The train had come from the north. Back at the wall, we limped north along a narrow road inside it, our spirits lifting a little as exercise warmed us. Beyond a bend, the railway ran out of a tunnel, across a long steel bridge over a cliff-rimmed gorge the stream had cut, and into our prison through a narrow archway in the barrier.

"We'd have to walk the bridge." Pepe stopped uneasily to shake his head at the ribbon of water on the canyon's rocky floor, far below. "A train could catch us on the track."

"We'll just wait for it to pass," Casey said.

We waited, lying hidden in a drainage ditch beside the track till the engine burst out of the tunnel, steam whistle howling. The cars rattled past us, riders leaning to stare at Sandor's restorations ahead. We clambered out of the ditch and sprinted across the bridge. Jumping off the track at the tunnel mouth, we rolled down a grass slope, got our breath, and tramped southwest away from the wall and into country that looked open.

The memorial sank behind a wooded ridge until all we could see was Sandor's replica of our own lookout dome on his replica of Tycho's rugged rim. We came out across a wide valley floor, scattered with clumps of trees and grazing animals I recognized; wildebeest, gazelles, and a little herd of graceful impala.

"Thanks to old Calvin DeFort. Another Noah saving Earth from a different deluge." Casey shaded his eyes to watch a pair of ostriches running from us across the empty land. "But where are the people?"

"Where's any water?" Pepe muttered. "No deluge, please. Just water we can drink."

We plodded on through tall green grass till I saw elephants marching out of a stand of trees off to our right. A magnificent bull with great white tusks, half a dozen others behind him, a baby with its mother. They came straight toward us. I wanted to run, but Casey simply beckoned for us to move aside. They ambled past us to drink from a pool we hadn't seen. Waiting till they had moved on, we turned toward the pool. Pepe pushed ahead and bent to scoop water up in his cupped hands.

"Don't!" a child's voice called behind us. "Unclean water might harm you."

A small girl came running toward us from the trees where the elephants had been. The first child we had seen, she was daintily lovely in a white blouse and a short blue skirt, her fair face half hidden under a wide-brimmed hat tied under her chin with a bright red ribbon.

"Hello." She stopped a few yards away, her blue eyes wide with wonder. "You are the Moon men?"

"And strangers here." Casey gave her our names. "Strangers in trouble."

"You deceived the ancient spaceship," she accused us soberly. "You should not be here on Earth."

We gaped at her. "How did you know?"

"The ship informed my father."

We stood silent, lost in wonder of our own. A charming picture of childish innocence, but she had shaken me with a chill of terror. Pepe stepped warily back from her, but after a moment Casey caught his breath to ask, "Who is your father?"

"You called him your uncle when you knew him on the Moon." Pride lit her face. "He is a very great and famous man. He discovered the lunar site and recovered the lost history of humankind. He rebuilt the ancient structures you saw around you where the ship came down."

"I get it." Casey nodded, looking crestfallen and dazed. "I think I begin to get it."

"We can't be sorry." Blinking at her, Pepe caught a long breath. "We'd had too much of the Moon. But now we're lost here, in a world I don't begin to understand. Do you know what will happen to us?"

"My father isn't sure." She looked away toward the replicated Tycho dome. "I used to beg him to take me with him to the Moon. He said the station had no place for me." She turned to study us again. "You are interesting to see. My name is—"

She uttered a string of rhythmic consonants and singing vowels, and smiled at Pepe's failure when he tried to imitate them.

"Just call me Tling," she said. "That will be easier for you to say." She turned to Pepe. "If you want water, come with me."

We followed her back to a little circle of square stones in the shade of the nearest tree. Beckoning us to sit, she opened a basket, found a bottle of water, and filled a cup for Pepe. Amused at the eager way he drained it, she filled it again for him, and then for Casey and me.

"I came out to visit the elephants," she told us. "I love elephants. I am very grateful to you Moon people for preserving the tissue specimens that have kept so many ancient creatures alive."

I had caught a tantalizing fragrance when she opened the basket. She saw Pepe's eyes still on it.

"I brought food for some of my forest friends," she said. "If you are hungry."

Pepe said we were starving. She spread a white napkin on one of the stones and began laying out what she had brought. Fruits I thought were peachlike and grapelike and pearlike, but wonderfully sweet and different. Small brown cakes with aromas that wet my mouth. We devoured them so avidly that she seemed amused.

"Where are the people?" Casey waved his arm at the empty landscape. "Don't you have cities?"

"We do," she said. "Though my father says they are smaller than those you built on the prehistoric Earth." She gestured toward the elephants. "We share the planet with other beings. He says you damaged it when you let your own biology run out of control."

"Maybe we did, but that's not what brought the impactor." Casey frowned again. "You are the only child we have seen."

"There's not much room for us. You see, we don't die."

I was listening, desperately hoping for something that might help us find or make a place for ourselves, but everything I heard was making our new world stranger. Casey gazed at her.

"Why don't you die?"

"If I can explain—" She paused as if looking for an answer we might understand. "My father says I should tell you that we have changed ourselves since the clones came back to colonize the dead Earth. We have altered the genes and invented the nanorobs."

"Nanorobs?"

She paused again, staring at the far-off elephants.

"My father calls them artificial symbiotes. They are tiny things that live like bacteria in our bodies but do good instead of harm. They are partly organic, partly diamond, partly gold. They move in the blood to repair or replace injured cells, or regrow a missing organ. They assist our nerves and our brain cells."

The food forgotten, we were staring at her. A picture of innocent simplicity in the simple skirt and blouse and floppy hat, she was suddenly so frightening that I trembled. She reached to put her small hand on mine before she went on.

"My father says I should say they are tiny robots, half-machine and half-alive. They are electronic. They can be programmed to store digital information. They pulse in unison, making their own waves in the brain and turning the whole body into a radio antenna. Sitting here speaking to you, I can also speak to my father."

She looked up to smile at me, her small hand closing on my fingers.

"Mr. Dunk, please don't be afraid of me. I know we seem different. I know I seem strange to you, but I would never harm you."

She was so charming that I wanted to take her in my arms, but my awe had grown to dread. We all shrank from her and sat wordless till hunger drove us to attack the fruit and cakes again. Pepe began asking questions as we ate.

Where did she live?

"On that hill." She nodded toward the west, but I couldn't tell which hill she meant. "My father selected a place where he could look out across the memorial."

Did she go to school?

"School?" The word seemed to puzzle her for a moment, and then she shook her head. "We do not require the schools my father says you had in the prehistoric world. He says your schools existed to program the brains of young people. Our nanocoms can be programmed and reprogrammed instantly, with no trouble at all, to load whatever information we need. That is how I learned your English when I needed it."

She smiled at his dazed face and selected a plump purple berry for herself.

"Our bodies, however, do need training." Delicately, she wiped her lips on a white napkin. "We form social groups to play games or practice skills. We fly our sliders all around the Earth. I love to ski on high mountains where snow falls. I've dived off coral reefs to observe sea things. I like music, art, drama, games of creation."

"That should be fun." Pepe's eyes were wide. "More fun than life in our tunnels on the Moon." His face went suddenly dark. "I hope your father doesn't send us back there."

"He can't, even if he wanted to." She laughed at his alarm. "He's finally done with the excavation. The charter site is closed and protected for future ages. All intrusion prohibited."

"So what will he do with us?"

"Does he have to do anything?" Seeming faintly vexed, she looked off toward the station dome on the crater ridge. "He says he has no place ready for you, but there are humanoid replicates playing your roles there in the Tycho simulation. I suppose you could replace them, if that would make you happy."

"Pretending we were back on the Moon?" Casey turned grim. "I don't think so."

"If you don't want that—"

She stopped, tipped her head as if to listen, and began gathering the water bottle and the rest of the fruit into the basket. Anxiously, Pepe asked if something was wrong.

"My mother." Frowning, she shook her head. "She's calling me home."

"Please!" Casey begged her. "Can't you stay a little longer? You are the only friend we've found. I don't know what we can do without you."

"I wish I could help you, but my mother is afraid for me."

"I wondered if you weren't in danger." He glanced out across the valley. "We saw a lion. Your really shouldn't be out here alone."

"It's not the lion." She shook her head. "I know him. A wonderful friend, so fast and strong and fierce." Her eyes shone at the recollection. "And I know a Bengal tiger. He was hiding in the brush because he was afraid of people. I taught him that we would never hurt him. Once he let me ride him when he chased a gazelle. It was wonderfully exciting."

Her voice grew solemn.

"I'm glad the gazelle got away, though the tiger was hungry and very disappointed. I try to forgive him, because I know he has to kill for food, like all the lions and leopards. They must kill, to stay alive. My mother says it is the way of nature, and entirely necessary. Too many grazing things would destroy the grass and finally starve themselves."

We stared again, wondering at her.

"How did you tame the tiger?"

"I think the nanorobs help me reach his mind, the way I touch yours. He learned that I respect him. We are good friends. He would fight to protect me, even from you."

"Is your mother afraid of us?"

She picked up the basket and stood shifting on her feet, frowning at us uncertainly.

"The nanorobs—" She hesitated. "I trust you, but the nanorobs—"

She stopped again.

"I thought you said nanorobs were good."

"That's the problem." She hesitated, trouble on her face. "My mother says you have none. She can't reach your minds. You do not hear when she speaks to you. She says you don't belong, because you are not one of us. What she fears—what she fears is you."

Speechless, Casey blinked at her sadly.

"I am sorry to go so soon." With a solemn little bow for each of us, she shook our hands. "Sorry you have no nanorobs. Sorry my mother is so anxious. Sorry to say good-bye."

"Please tell your father—" Casey began.

"He knows," she said. "He is sorry you came here."

Walking away with her basket, she turned to wave her hand at us, her face framed for a moment by the wide-brimmed hat. I thought she was going to speak, but in a moment she was gone.

"Beautiful!" Casey whispered. "She'll grow up to be another Mona."

Looking back toward the copied monuments of the old Earth, the copied station dome shining on the copied Tycho rim, I saw a dark-maned lion striding across the valley toward the pool where the elephants had drunk. Three smaller females followed. None of them our friends. I shivered.

5

WE WANDERED ON UP the valley after Tling left us, keeping clear of the trees and trying to stay alert for danger or any hint of help.

"If Sandor lives out here," Casey said, "there must be others. People, I hope, who won't take us for robots."

We stopped to watch impala drinking at a water hole. They simply raised their heads to look at us, but fled when a cheetah burst out of a thicket. The smallest was too slow. The cheetah knocked it down and carried it back into the brush.

"No nanorobs for them," Pepe muttered. "Or us."

We tramped on, finding no sign of anything human. By mid-afternoon, hungry and thirsty again, with nothing human in view ahead, we sat down to rest on an outcropping of rock. Pepe dug a little holo of Tanya out of his breast pocket and passed it to show us her dark-eyed smile.

"If we hadn't lost the radio—" He caught himself, with a stiff little grin. "Still, I guess we wouldn't call. I'd love to hear her voice. I know she's anxious, but I wouldn't want her to know the fix we're in—"

He stopped when a shadow flickered across the holo. Looking up, we found a silvery slider craft dropping to the grass a few yards from us. An oval door dilated in the side of it. Tling jumped out.

"We found you!" she cried. "Even with no nanorobs. Here is my mother."

A slender woman came out behind her, laughing at Pepe when he tried to repeat the name she gave us.

"She says you can just call her Lo."

Tling still wore the blouse and skirt, with her wide-brimmed hat, but Lo was nude except for a gauzy blue sash worn over her shoulder. As graceful and trim, and nearly as sexless as Sandor, she had the same cream-colored skin, already darkening where the sun struck it, but she had a thick crown of bright red-brown curls instead of Sandor's cap of sleek fur.

"Dr. Yare." Tling spoke carefully to let us hear. "Mr. Navarro. Mr. Kell, who is also called El Chino. They were cloned at Tycho Station from prehistoric tissue specimens."

"You were cloned for duty there." Lo eyed us severely. "How did you get here?"

"We lied to the ship." Casey straightened wryly to face her. "We did it because we didn't want to live out our lives in that pit on the Moon. I won't say I'm sorry, but now we are in trouble. I don't want to die."

"You will die," she told him bluntly. "Like all your kind. You carry no nanorobs."

"I guess." He shrugged. "But first we want a chance to live."

"Mother, please!" Tling caught her hand. "With no nanorobs, they are in immediate danger here. Can we help them stay alive?"

"That depends on your father."

"I tried to ask him," Tling said. "He didn't answer."

We watched Lo's solemn frown, saw Tling's deepening trouble.

"I wish you had nanorobs." She turned at last to translate for us. "My father has gone out to meet an interstellar ship that has just come back after eight hundred years away. The officers are telling him a very strange story."

She looked up at her mother, as if listening.

"It carried colonists for the planets of the star Enthel, which is four hundred light-years toward the galactic core. They had taken off with no warning of trouble. The destination planet had been surveyed and opened for settlement. It had rich natural resources, with no native life to be protected. Navigation algorithms for the flight had been tested, occupation priorities secured."

She stared up at the sky, in baffled dismay.

"Now the ship has returned, two thousand colonists still aboard."

Casey asked what had gone wrong. We waited, watching their anxious frowns.

"My father is inquiring." Tling turned back to us. "He's afraid of something dreadful."

"It must have been dreadful," Pepe whispered. "Imagine eight hundred years on a ship in space!"

"Only instants for them." Tling shook her head, smiling at him. "Time stops, remember, at the speed of light. By their own time, they left only yesterday. Yet their situation is still hard enough. Their friends are scattered away. Their whole world is gone. They feel lost and desperate."

She turned to her mother. "Why couldn't they land?"

Her mother listened again. Far out across the valley I saw a little herd of zebras running. I couldn't see what had frightened them.

"My father is asking," she told us at last. "The passengers were not told why the ship had to turn back. The officers have promised a statement, but my father says they can't agree on what to say. They aren't sure what they found on the destination planet. He believes they're afraid to say what they believe."

The running zebras veered aside. I saw the tawny flash of a lion charging to meet them, saw a limping zebra go down. My own ankle was aching from a stone that had turned under my foot, and I felt as helpless as the zebra.

"Don't worry, Mr. Dunk." Tling reached to touch my arm. "My father is very busy with the ship. I don't know what he can do with you, but I don't want the animals to kill you. I think we can keep you safe till he comes home. Can't we, mother?"

Her lips pressed tight, Lo shrugged as if she had forgotten us.

"Please, mother. I know they are primitives, but they would never harm me. I can understand them the way I understand the animals. They are hungry and afraid, with nowhere else to go."

Lo stood motionless for a moment, frowning at us.

"Get in."

She beckoned us into the flyer and lifted her face again as if listening to the sky.

We soared toward a rocky hill and landed on a level ledge near the summit. Climbing out, we looked down across the grassy valley and over the ridge to Sandor's memorial just beyond. Closer than I expected, I found the bright metal glint of the rebuilt spaceplane on the mall, the Capitol dome and the Washington obelisk, the white marble sheen of the Egyptian pyramid looming out of green forest beyond.

"My father picked this spot." Tling nodded toward the cliff. "He wanted to watch the memorial built."

While her mother stood listening intently at the sky, Tling inspected our mudstained safari suits.

"You need a bath," she decided, "before you eat."

Running ahead, she took us down an arched tunnel into the hill and showed me into a room far larger than my cell below the station dome. Warm water sprayed me when I stepped into the shower, warm air dried me. A human-shaped robot handed me my clothing when I came out, clean and neatly folded. It guided me to a room where Tling was already sitting with Pepe and Casey at a table set with plates around a pyramid of fragrant fruit.

"Mr. Chino asked about my mother." She looked up to smile at me. "You saw that she's different, with different nanorobs. She comes from the Garenkrake system, three hundred light-years away. Its people had forgotten where they came from. She wanted to know. When her search for the mother planet brought her here, she found my father already digging at the Tycho site. They've worked together ever since."

Pepe and Casey were already eating. Casey turned to Tling, who was nibbling delicately at something that looked like a huge purple orchid.

"What do you think will happen to us?"

"I'll ask my father when I can." She glanced toward the ceiling. "He is still busy with the ship's officers. I'm sorry you're afraid of my mother. She doesn't hate you, not really. If she seems cool to you, it's just because she has worked so long at the site, digging up relics of the first world. She thinks you seem so—so primitive."

She shook her head at our uneasy frowns.

"You told her you lied to the ship." She looked at Casey. "That bothers her, because the nanorobs do not transmit untruths or let people hurt each other. She feels sorry for you."

Pepe winced. "We feel sorry for ourselves."

Tling sat for a minute, silently, frowning, and turned back to us.

"The ship is big trouble for my father," she told us. "It leaves him no time for you. He says you should have stayed on the Moon."

"I know." Casey shrugged. "But we're here. We can't go back. We want to stay alive."

"I feel your fear." She gave us an uneasy smile. "My father's too busy to talk to you, but if you'll come to my room, there is news about the ship."

The room must have been her nursery. In one corner was a child's bed piled with dolls and toys, a cradle on the floor beside it. The wall above was alive with a scenic holo. Long-legged birds flew away from a water hole when a tiger came out of tall grass to drink. A zebra stallion ventured warily close, snuffing at us. A prowling leopard froze and ran from a bull elephant. She gestured at the wall.

"I was a baby here, learning to love the animals."

That green landscape was suddenly gone. The wall had become a wide window that showed us great spacecraft drifting though empty blackness. Blinding highlights glared where the Sun struck it. The rest was lost in shadow, but I made out a thick bright metal disk, slowly turning. Tiny-looking sliders clung around a bulging dome at its center.

"It's in parking orbit, waiting for anywhere to go," Tling said. "Let's look inside."

She gave us glimpses of the curving floors where the spin created a false gravity. People sat in rows of seats like those in holos of ancient aircraft. More stood crowded in aisles and corridors. I heard scraps of hushed and anxious talk.

"...home on a Pacific island."

The camera caught a woman with a crown of what looked like bright golden feathers instead of hair. Holding a whimpering baby in one arm, the other around a grim-faced man, she was answering questions from someone we didn't see. The voice we heard was Tling's.

"It's hard for us." Her lips were not moving, but the voice went sharp with her distress. "We had a good life there. Mark's an imagineer. I was earning a good living as a genetic artist, designing ornamentals to special order. We are not the pioneer type, but we did want a baby." An ironic wry smile twisted her lips. "A dream come true!"

She lifted the infant to kiss its gold-capped head.

"Look at us now." She smiled sadly at the child. "We spent our savings for a vision of paradise on Fendris Four. A tropical beachfront be-

tween the surf and a bamboo forest, snow on a Volcanic cone behind it.
A hundred families of us, all friends forever."

She sighed and rocked the baby.

"They didn't let us off the ship. Or even tell us why. We're desperate,
with our money gone and baby to care for. Now they say there's nowhere
else we can go."

The wall flickered and the holos came back with monkeys chattering
in jungle treetops.

"That's the problem," Tling said. "Two thousand people like them,
stuck on the ship with nowhere to live. My father's problem now, since
the council voted to put him in charge."

Casey asked, "Why can't they leave the ship?"

"If you don't understand—" She was silent for a moment. "My mother
says it's the way of the nanorobs. They won't let people overrun the planet and use it up like my mother says the primitives did, back before the
impacts. Births must be balanced by migration. Those unlucky people
lost their space when they left Earth."

"Eight hundred years ago?"

"Eight hundred of our time." She shrugged. "A day or so of theirs."

"What can your father do for them?"

"My mother says he's still searching for a safe destination."

"If he can't find one—" Casey frowned. "And they can't come home. It
seems terribly unfair. Do you let the nanorobs rule you?"

"Rule us?" Puzzled, she turned her head to listen and nodded at the
wall. "You don't understand. They do unite us, but there is no conflict.
They live in all of us, acting to keep us alive and well, guiding us to stay
free and happy, but moving us only by our own consent. My mother says
they are part of what you used to call the unconscious."

"Those people on the ship?" Doubtfully, Casey frowned. "Still alive, I
guess, but not free to get off or happy at all."

"They are troubled." Nodding soberly she listened again. "But my
mother says I should explain the nanorob way. She says the old primitives
lived in what she calls the way of the jungle genes, back when survival
required traits of selfish aggression. The nanorobs have let us change our
genes to escape the greed and jealousy and violence that led to so much
crime and war and pain on the ancient Earth. They guide us toward what
is best for all. My mother says the people on the ship will be content to
follow the nanorob way when my father has helped them find it."

She turned her head. "I heard my mother call."

I hadn't heard a thing, but she ran out of the room. In the holo wall, high-shouldered wildebeest were leaping off a cliff to swim across a river. One stumbled, toppled, vanished under the rapid water. We watched in dismal silence till Casey turned to frown at Pepe and me.

"I don't think I like the nanorob way."

We had begun to understand why Sandor had no place on Earth for us.

6

"DEAR SIRS, I MUST BEG you to excuse us."

Tling made a careful little bow and explained that her mother was taking her to dance and music practice, then going on to a meeting about the people on the stranded ship. We were left alone with the robots. They were man-shaped, ivory-colored, blank-faced. Lacking nanorobs, they were voice-controlled.

Casey tried to question them about the population, cities, and industries of the new Earth, but they had been programmed only for domestic service, with no English or information about anything else. Defeated by their blank-lensed stares, we sat out on the terrace, looking down across the memorial and contemplating our own uncertain future, till they called us in for dinner.

The dishes they served us were strange, but Pepe urged us to eat while we could.

"¿Mañana?" He shook his head uneasily. "¿Quién sabe?"

Night was falling before we got back to the terrace. A thin Moon was setting in the west. In the east, a locomotive headlight flashed across the memorial. The mall was lit for evening tours, the Taj Mahal a glowing gem, the Great Pyramid an ivory island in the creeping dusk. The robots had our beds ready when the light went out. They had served wine with dinner, and I slept without a dream.

Awake early next morning, rested again and lifted with unreasonable hope, I found Tling standing outside at the end of the terrace, looking down across the valley. She had hair like her mother's, not feathers or fur, but blonde and cropped short. Despite the awesome power of her nanorobs, I thought she looked very small and vulnerable. She started when I spoke.

"Good morning, Mr. Dunk." She wiped at her face with the back of her hand and tried to smile. I saw that her eyes were puffy and red. "How is your ankle?"

"Better."

"I was worried." She found a pale smile. "Because you have no symbiotes to help repair such injuries."

I asked if she had heard from her father and the emigrant ship. She turned silently to look again across the sunlit valley and the memorial. I saw the far plume of steam from an early train crawling over the bridge toward the Sphinx.

"I watched a baby giraffe." Her voice was slow and faint, almost as if she was speaking to herself. "I saw it born. I watched it learning to stand, nuzzling its mother, learning to suck. It finally followed her away, wobbling on its legs. It was beautiful—"

Her voice failed. Her hand darted to her lips. She stood trembling, staring at me, her eyes wide and dark with pain.

"My father!" Her voice came suddenly sharp and thin, almost a scream. "He's going away. I'll never see him again."

She ran back inside.

When the robots called us to breakfast, we found her sitting between her parents. She had washed her tear-streaked face, but the food on her plate had not been touched. Here out of the Sun, Sandor's face had gone pale and grim. He seemed not to see us till Tling turned to frown at him. He rose then, and came around the table to shake our hands.

"Good morning, Dr. Pen." Casey gave him a wry smile. "I see why you didn't want us here, but I can't apologize. We'll never be sorry we came."

"Sit down." He spoke shortly. "Let's eat."

We sat. The robots brought us plates loaded with foods we had never tasted. Saying no more to us, Sandor signaled a robot to refill his cup of the bitter black tea and bent over a bowl of crimson berries. Tling sat looking up at him in anguished devotion till Casey spoke.

"Sir, we heard about your problem with the stranded colonists. Can you tell us why their ship came back?"

"Nothing anybody understands." He shook his head and gave Tling a tender smile before he pushed the berries aside and turned gravely back to us. His voice was quick and crisp. "The initial survey expedition had found their destination planet quite habitable and seeded it with terran-type life. Expeditions had followed to settle the three major continents. This group was to find room on the third.

"They arrived safe but got no answer when they called the planet from orbit. The atmosphere was hazed with dust that obscured the surface, but a search in the infrared found relics of a very successful occupa-

tion. Pavements, bridges, masonry, steel skeletons that had been buildings. All half buried under dunes of red, windblown dust. No green life
anywhere. A derelict craft from one of the pioneer expeditions was still
in orbit, but dead as the planet.

"They never learned what killed the planet. No news of the disaster
seems to have reached any other world, which suggests that it struck un-
expectedly and spread fast. The medical officers believe the killer may have
been some unknown organism that attacks organic life, but the captain
refused to allow any attempt to land or investigate. She elected to turn
back at once, without contact. A choice that probably saved their lives."

He picked up his spoon and bent again to his bowl of berries. I tried
one of them. It was tart, sweet, with a heady tang I can't describe.

"Sir," Casey spoke again, "we saw those people. They're desperate.
What will happen to them now?"

"A dilemma." Sandor looked at Tling, with a sad little shrug. She
turned her head to hide a sob. "Habitable planets are relatively rare. The
few we find must be surveyed, terraformed, approved for settlement. As
events came out, these people have been fortunate. We were able to get
an emergency waiver that will allow them to settle on an open planet,
five hundred light-years in toward the core. Fuel and fresh supplies are
being loaded now."

"And my father—" Tling looked up at me, her voice almost a wail.
"He has to go with them. All because of me."

He put his arm around her and bent his face to hers. Whatever he
said was silent. She climbed into his arms. He hugged her, rocking her
back and forth like a baby, till her weeping ceased. With a smile that
broke my heart, she kissed him and slid out of his arms.

"Excuse us, please." Her voice quivering, she caught his hand. "We
must say good-bye."

She led him out of the room.

Lo stared silently after them till Pepe tapped his bowl to signal the
robots for a second serving of the crimson berries.

"It's true." With a long sigh, she turned back to us. "A painful thing
for Tling. For all three of us. This is not what we planned."

Absently, she took a little brown cake from a tray the robot was passing and laid it on her plate, untasted.

"¿Que tienes?" Pepe gave her a puzzled look.

"We hoped to stay together," she said. "Sandor and I have worked
here for most of the century, excavating the site and restoring what we

could. With that finished, I wanted to see my homeworld again. We were going back there together, Tling with us. Taking the history we had learned, we were planning to replicate the memorial there."

Bleakly, she shook her head.

"This changes everything. Sandor feels a duty to help the colonists find a home. Tling begged him to take us with him, but—" She shrugged in resignation, her lips drawn tight. "He's afraid of whatever killed Enthel Two. And there's something else. His brother—"

She looked away for a moment.

"He has a twin brother. His father had to emigrate when they were born. He took the twin. His mother had a career in nanorob genetics she couldn't leave. Sandor stayed here with her, longing for his twin. He left when he was grown, searched a dozen worlds, never found him. He did find me. That's the happy side."

Her brief smile faded.

"A hopeless quest, I've told him. There are too many worlds, too many light-years. Slider flights may seem quick, but they take too long. Yet he can't give up the dream."

"Can we—" Casey checked himself to look at Pepe and me. We nodded, and he turned anxiously back to Lo. "If Sandor does go out on the emigrant ship, would he take us with him?"

She shook her head and sat staring at nothing till Pepe asked, "*¿Por qué no?*"

"Reasons enough." Frowning, she picked up the little brown cake, broke it in half, dropped the fragments back on her plate. "First of all, the danger. Whatever killed that planet could kill another. He got the waiver, in fact, because others were afraid to go. The colonists had no choice, but he doesn't want to kill you."

"It's our choice." Casey shrugged. "When you have to jump across hundreds of years of space and time, don't you always take a risk?"

"Not like this one." She shrugged unhappily. "Enthel Two is toward the galactic core. So is this new one. If the killer is coming from the core—"

Pale face set, she shook her fair-haired head.

"We'll take the risk." Casey glanced again at us and gave her a stiff little grin. "You might remind him that we weren't cloned to live forever. He has more at stake than we do."

Her body stiffened, fading slowly white.

"Tling and I have begged him." Her voice was faint. "But he feels commanded."

"By his nanorobs? Can't he think of you and Tling?"

Her answer took a long time to come.

"You don't understand them." She seemed composed again; I wondered if her own nanorobs had eased her pain. "You may see them as micromachines, but they don't make us mechanical. We've kept all the feelings and impulses the primitives had. The nanorobs simply make us better humans. Sandor is going not just for the colonists, but for me and Tling, for people everywhere."

"If the odds are as bad as they look—" Casey squinted doubtfully. "What can one man hope to do?"

"Nothing, perhaps." She made a bleak little shrug. "But he has an idea. Long ago, before he ever left Earth to search for his brother, he worked with his mother on her nanorob research. He has reprogrammed himself with the science. If the killer is some kind of virulent organism, he thinks the nanorobs might be modified into a shield against it."

"Speak to him," Casey begged her. "Get him to take us with him. We'll help him any way we can."

"You?" Astonishment widened her eyes. "How?"

"We put you here on Earth," he told her. "Even with no nanorobs at all."

"So you did." Golden color flushed her skin. "I'll speak to him." Silent for a moment, she shook her head. "Impossible. He says every seat on the ship is filled."

She paused, frowning at the ceiling. The robot was moving around the table, offering a bowl of huge flesh-colored mushrooms that had a tempting scent of frying ham.

"We are trying to plan a future for Tling." Her face was suddenly tight, her voice hushed with feeling. "A thousand years will pass before he gets back. He grieves to leave Tling."

"I saw her this morning," I said. "She's terribly hurt."

"We are trying to make it up. I've promised that she will see him again."

Pepe looked startled. "How can that happen?"

She took a mushroom, sniffed it with a nod of approval, and laid it on her plate.

"We must plan the time," she told him. "Tling and I will travel. I want to see what the centuries have done to my own homeworld. It will take careful calculation and the right star flights, but we'll meet him back here on the date of his return."

"If—"

Casey swallowed his voice. Her face went pale, but after a moment she gave us a stiff little smile and had the robot offer the mushrooms again. They had a name I never learned, and a flavor more like bittersweet chocolate than ham. The meal ended. She left us there alone with the robots, with nowhere to go, no future in sight.

"A thousand years!" Pepe muttered. "I wish we had nanorobs."

"Or else—"

Casey turned to the door.

"News for you." Lo stood there, smiling at us. "News from the emigrant ship. Uneasy passengers have arranged for new destinations, leaving empty places. Sandor has found seats for you."

7

SANDOR TOOK US TO OUR SEATS on the emigrant ship. Wheel-shaped and slowly spinning, it held us to the floors with a force weaker than Earth's gravity, stronger than the Moon's. A blue light flashed to warn us of the space-time slide. Restraints folded around us. I felt a gut-wrenching tug. The restraints released us. With no sense of any other change, we sat uneasily waiting.

The big cabin was hushed. Watching faces, I saw eager expectation give way to disappointment and distress. I heard a baby crying, someone shouting at a robot attendant, then a rising clamor of voices at the brink of panic. Sandor sat looking gravely away till I asked him what was wrong.

"We don't know." He grinned at our dazed wonderment. "At least we've made the skip to orbit. Five hundred light-years. You're old men now."

He let us follow him to the lounge, where a tall ceiling dome imaged a new sky. The Milky Way looked familiar. I found the Orion Nebula, but all the nearer stars had shifted beyond recognition. I felt nothing from the ship's rotation; the whole sky seemed to turn around us. Two suns rose, set close together. One was yellow, smaller and paler than our own, the brighter a hot blue dazzle. The planet climbed behind them, a huge round blot on the field of unfamiliar stars, edged with the blue sun's glare. Looking for the glow of cities, all I saw was darkness.

Anxious passengers were clustering around crew members uniformed in the ship's blue-and-gold caps and sashes. Most of their questions were in the silent language of the nanorobs, but their faces revealed dismay. I heard voices rising higher, cries of shock and dread.

We turned to Sandor.

"The telescopes pick up no artificial lights." His lean face was bleakly set. "Radio calls get no answer. The electronic signal spectrum appears dead." He shook his head, with a heavy sigh. "I was thinking of my brother. I'd hoped to find him here."

With gestures of apology to us, uneasy people pushed to surround him. He looked away to listen, frowning at the planet's dark shadow, and turned forlornly to go. He spoke his final words for us.

"We'll be looking for survivors."

We watched that crescent of blue-and-orange fire widen with each passage across the ceiling dome till at last we saw the planet's globe. Swirls and streamers of high cloud shone brilliantly beneath the blue sun's light, but thick red dust dulled everything under them.

One hemisphere was all ocean, except for the gray dot of an isolated island. A single huge continent covered most of the other, extending far south of the equator and north across the pole. Mountain ranges walled the long west coast. A single giant river system drained the vast valley eastward. From arctic ice to polar sea it was all rust-red, nothing green anywhere.

"A rich world it must have been." Sandor made a dismal shrug. "But now—?"

He turned to nod at a woman marching into the room. A woman so flat-chested, masculine, and strange that I had to look twice. Gleaming red-black scales covered her angular body, even her hairless head. Her face was a narrow triangle, her chin sharply pointed, her eyes huge and green. We stared as she sprang to a circular platform in the center of the room.

"Captain Vlix," he murmured. "She's older than I am, born back in the days when nanorobs were new and body forms experimental. I sailed with her once. She remembered my brother asking if she knew me. That was Earth centuries ago. She had no clues to give me."

Heads were turning in attention. I saw uneasy expectation give way to bitter disappointment. Sandor stood frozen, widened eyes fixed on her, till she turned to meet another officer joining her on the platform. They conferred in silence.

"What is it?" Casey whispered. Sandor seemed deaf till Casey touched his arm and asked again, "What did she say?"

"Nothing good." Sandor turned to us, his voice hushed and hurried. "She was summing up a preliminary report from the science staff. This dead planet is the second they have reached. The other was two hundred light-years away. The implications—"

He hunched his shoulders, his skin gone pale.

"Yes? What are they?"

With a painful smile, he tried to gather himself.

"At this point, only speculation. The killer has reached two worlds. How many more? Its nature is not yet known. The science chief suggests that it could possibly be a malignant nanorob, designed to attack all organic life. It certainly seems aggressive, advancing on an interstellar front from the direction of the galactic core."

"What can we do?"

"Nothing, unless we come to understand it." He glanced at the captain and spread his empty hands. "Nanorobs are designed to survive and reproduce themselves. They are complex, half alive, half machine, more efficient than either. The early experimenters worked in terror of accident, of creating something malignant that might escape the laboratory. This could be a mutation. It could be a weapon, reprogrammed by some madman—though his own nanorobs should have prevented that."

He looked again at the captain, and slowly shook his head.

"The officers are doing what they can. A robotic drone is being prepared to attempt a low-level survey of surface damage. A search has already begun for any spacecraft that might remain in orbit. And—"

He broke off to watch a thin man with a gray cap and sash who darted out of the crowd and jumped to join the officers on the platform.

"That's Benkar Rokehut." He made a wry face. "A fellow Earthman, born in my own century. A noted entrepreneur, or perhaps I should say gambler. Noted for taking unlikely chances. He has opened half a dozen worlds, made and lost a dozen fortunes. He funded the initial surveys and settlements here. He has a fortune at stake."

His golden shoulders tossed to an ironic shrug.

"He may love wild chances, but he doesn't want to die."

Rokehut faced the captain for a moment, and turned silently to address the room. Gesturing at the planet, pointing at features on the surface, he kept turning to follow as it crept overhead, kept on talking. When Captain Vlix moved as if to stop him, he burst suddenly into speech, shouting vehemently at her, his pale skin flushing redder than the planet.

"His emotions have overcome his nanorobs." Sandor frowned and drew us closer. "All he sees is danger. Though that first lost planet is two hundred light-years from this one, they both lie toward the Core from Earth. He believes the killer pathogen is spreading from somewhere toward the Core, possibly carried by refugees. He wants us to head out for the frontier stars toward the Rim."

The officers moved to confront him. What they said was silent, but I saw Rokehut's face fade almost to the gray of his cap and sash. He snatched them off, threw them off the platform, waved his fists and shouted. Yielding at last, he shuffled aside and stood glaring at Captain Vlix, his fists still clenched with a purely human fury.

She turned silently back to face the room, speaking with a calm control.

"The officers agree that we do seem to face an interstellar invasion." Sandor spoke softly. "But blind flight can only spread the contagion, if panicky refugees carry it. In the end, unless we get some better break—"

With a sad little shrug, he paused to look hard at us.

"Tycho Station could become the last human hope. It is sealed, shielded, well concealed. The Moon has no surface life to attract or sustain any kind of pathogen." His lips twisted to a quirk of bitter humor. "Even if it wins, there's hope for humanity. It should die when no hosts are left to carry it. You clones may have another book to write before your epic ends."

Captain Vlix left the room, Rokehut and his people close behind her. The robot attendants were circulating with trays of hard brown biscuits and plastic bubbles of fruit juice.

"The best we can do," Sandor said. "With zero times in transit, the ship carries no supplies or provisions for any prolonged stay aboard. We must move on with no long delay, yet the officers agree that we must wait for whatever information we can get from the drone."

It descended over the glaciers that fringed the polar cap and flew south along the rugged west coast. Its cameras projected their images on the dome and the edge of the floor. Standing there, I could feel that I was riding in its nose. It must have flown high and fast, but the images were processed to make it seem that we hovered low and motionless over a deserted seaport or the ruin of a city and climbed to soar on to the next.

All we saw was dust and desolation. Broken walls of stone or brick, where roofs had fallen in. Tangles of twisted steel where towers had stood. Concrete seawalls around empty harbors. And everywhere, wind-drifted dunes of dead red dust and wind-whipped clouds of rust-colored dust, sometimes so dense it hid the ground.

The drone turned east near the equator, climbing over mountain peaks capped with snows dyed the color of drying blood. It paused over broken dams in high mountain canyons and crossed a network of dust-choked irrigation canals.

"I've dreamed of my brother." Sandor made a solemn face. "Dreamed I might find him here." He stopped to sigh and gaze across an endless sea of wave-shaped dunes. "Dreams! All of us dreaming we had endless life and time for everything. And now—"

The drone had reached the dead east coast and flown on across the empty ocean. The lounge was silent again, disheartened people drifting away. Casey asked if we were turning back.

"Not quite yet." Sandor tipped his head, listening. "Captain Vlix reports that the search team has found something in low polar orbit. Maybe a ship. Maybe just a rock. Maybe something else entirely. She's launching a pilot pod to inspect it."

Music had lifted back in the lounge, its unfamiliar trills and runs and strains broken by long gaps of nothing I could sense. A woman with a baby in her arms was swaying to a rhythm I couldn't hear. Silent people were dozing or wandering the aisles. A silent group had gathered around Rokehut at the end of the room, frowning and gesticulating.

"He still wants us to run for our lives," Sandor said. "For a star two thousand light-years out toward the Rim. An idiot's dream! To complete the slide he'd have to calculate the exact relative position of the star two thousand years from now. He has no data for it."

The attendants came back with juice and little white wafers. Rokehut and his group refused them, with angry gestures, and trooped away to confront the captain again.

"A mild sedative." Sandor waved the robot away. "If you need to relax."

I accepted a wafer. It had a vinegar taste and it hit me with a sudden fatigue. I slept in my seat till Casey shook my arm.

"The pod has reached that object in orbit," Sandor told us. "The pilot identifies it as the craft that brought the last colonists. His attempts at contact get no response. Rokehut has offered him a fortune to go aboard. Permission has been granted, with the warning that he won't be allowed back on our ship. He reports that his service robot is now cutting the security bolts to let him into the air lock."

I watched the people around us, silently listening, frowning intently, expectantly nodding, frowning again.

"He's inside." Head tipped aside, eyes fixed on something far away, Sandor spoke at last. "The pathogen got there ahead of him. He has found red dust on the decks, but he hopes for protection from his space gear. He believes the killer was already on the planet before the ship arrived. The cargo was never unloaded. All organics have crumbled, but metal remains unchanged.

"He's pushing on—"

Sandor stopped to listen and shake his head.

"The pilot was on his way to the control room, searching for records or clues. He never got there." He leaned his head and nodded. "The science chief is summing up what evidence he has. It points to something airborne, fast-acting, totally lethal. It must have killed everybody who ever knew what it is."

Captain Vlix allowed Rokehut and his partisans to poll the passengers. Overwhelmingly, they voted to turn back toward Earth at once. The lounge became a bedlam of angry protest when departure was delayed, hushed a little when Captain Vlix came back to the platform.

"She says Earth is out," Sandor told us, "for two sufficient reasons. We might find that the pathogen is already there. Even if we found it safe, she says we would certainly be regarded as a suspected carrier, warned away and subject to attack if we tried to make any contact."

"That recalls a legend of the old Earth." Casey nodded bleakly. "The legend of a ghost ship called the Flying Dutchman, that sailed forever and never reached a port."

The strange constellations flickered out of the ceiling dome, and the drone's images returned. The limitless ocean beneath it looked blue as Earth's when we glimpsed it through rifts in the clouds, but the sky was yellow, the larger sun a sullen red, the blue one now a hot pink point.

"The island's somewhere ahead." Sandor stood with us in the lounge, frowning at the horizon. "If we ever get there. It's losing altitude. Losing speed. Probably damaged by the dust."

White-capped waves rose closer as it glided down through scattered puffs of cumulus.

"There it is!" Sandor whispered before I had seen it. "Just to the right."

I strained to see. The image dimmed and flickered as the drone bored through a tuft of pink-tinted cloud. Something blurred the far horizon. At first a faint dark streak, it faded and came back as we searched it for color.

"Green?" A sharp cry from Casey. "Isn't it green?"

"It was," Sandor said. "We're going down."

A foam-capped mountain of blue-green water climbed ahead of the drone. It crashed with an impact I almost felt, but I thought I had caught a flash of green.

8

THE CEILING DOME HAD GONE DARK when the drone broke up. After a moment it was spangled again with those new constellations. The dead ship, immense and high overhead, was a fire-edged silhouette against the Milky Way.

"You saw it!" Casey shouted at Sandor. "Something green. Something alive!"

Frowning, Sandor shook his head.

"I saw a brief greenish flash. Probably from some malfunction as the drone went down."

"It was green," Casey insisted. "Aren't they landing anybody to take a look?"

"No time for that."

"But if the island is alive—"

"How could that be?" He was sharply impatient. "We've seen the whole planet dead. Whatever killed it killed the drone before it ever touched the surface. The captain isn't going to risk any sort of contact."

"If she would let us land—" Casey waited for Pepe and me to nod. "We could radio a report."

"Send you down to die?" Sandor's eyes went wide. "She cares too much for life. She would never consider it."

"Don't think we care for life? Tell her we were cloned to keep the Earth and humankind alive. But tell her we were also cloned to die. If we must, I don't know a better way."

Sandor took us to meet Captain Vlix, and translated for us. Our visit was brief, but still enough to let me glimpse a spark of humanity beneath her gleaming crimson scales. I don't know what he told her, but it caught her interest. She had him question us about Tycho Station and our lives there.

"You like it?" Her huge green eyes probed us with a disturbing intensity. "Life without nanorobs? Knowing you must die?"

"We know." Casey nodded. "I don't dwell on it."

"I must admire your idealism." A frown creased her crimson scales. "But the science staff reports no credible evidence of life on the planet. I can't waste your lives."

"We saw evidence we believe," Casey said. "In that last second as the drone went down. Considering the stakes, we're ready to take the risk."

"The stakes are great." Her eyes on Sandor, she frowned and finally nodded her red-scaled head. "You may go."

There were no space suits to fit us. That didn't matter, Casey said; space gear had not saved the pilot who boarded the derelict. With Sandor translating, the service robots showed Pepe how to operate the flight pod, a streamlined bubble much like the slider that had brought Sandor to the Moon. He shook our hands and wished us well.

"Make it quick," he told us. "Captain Vlix expects no good news from you. No news at all, in fact, after you touch down. Our next destination is still under debate. None looks safe, or satisfies everybody, but we can't delay."

Pepe made it quick, and we found the island green.

Rising out of the haze of dust as we dived, the shallow sea around it faded from the blue of open water through a hundred shades of jade and turquoise to the vivid green of life. The island was bowl-shaped, the great caldera left by an ancient volcanic explosion. Low hills rimmed a circular valley with a small blue lake at the center. A line of green trees showed the course of a stream that ran through a gap in the hills from the lake down to the sea.

"Kell?" Sandor's voice crackled from the radio before we touched the ground. "Navarro? Yare? Answer if you can."

"Tell him!" Casey grinned at Pepe as he dropped our slider pod to a wide white beach that looked like coral sand. "It looks a lot better than our pits in the Moon. No matter what."

Pepe echoed him, "No matter what."

"Tell him we're opening the air lock," Casey said. "If we can breathe the air, we're heading inland."

Pepe opened the air lock. I held my breath till I had to inhale. The air was fresh and cool, but I caught a faint acrid bite. In a moment my eyes were burning. Pepe sneezed and clapped a handkerchief over his nose. Casey smothered a cough and peered at us sharply.

"Can you report?" Sandor's anxious voice. "Can you breathe?"

Casey coughed and blew his nose.

"Breathing," he gasped. "Still breathing."

I thought we were inhaling the pathogen. I hadn't known the pilot who died on the derelict, or the millions or billions it had killed. I felt no personal pain for them, but Pepe and Casey were almost part of me. I put my arms around them. We huddled there together, sneezing and wheezing, till Pepe laughed and pulled away.

"If this is death, it ain't so bad." He jogged me in the ribs. "Let's get out and take a closer look."

We stumbled out of the lock and stood there on the hard wet sand beside the pod, breathing hard and peering around us. The sky was a dusty pink, the suns a tiny red moon eye and a bright pink spark. The beach sloped up to low green hills. Perhaps half a mile south along the beach, green jungle covered the delta at the mouth of the little river. Pepe picked up a scrap of seaweed the waves had left.

"Still green." He studied it, sniffed it. "It smells alive."

My lungs were burning. Every breath, I thought, might be my last, yet I always stayed able to struggle for another. Pepe dropped the handkerchief and climbed back in the slider to move it higher on the beach, farther from the water. He returned with a portable radio. Casey blew his nose again, and started south along the beach, toward the delta. We followed him, breathing easier as we went.

The little river had cut its way between two great black basaltic cliffs. Casey stopped before we reached them, frowning up at the nearest. I looked and caught a deeper breath. The summit had been carved into a face. The unfinished head of a giant struggling out of the stone.

"Sandor!" Casey walked closer, staring up at the great dark face. "It's Sandor."

"It is." Shading his eyes, Pepe whispered huskily. "Unless we're crazy."

I had to sneeze again, and wondered what the dust was doing to us.

Sandor called again from the ship, but Pepe seemed too stunned to speak. A rope ladder hung across the face, down to the beach. Black and gigantic, gazing out at the sky, lips curved in a puckish smile, the head was certainly Sandor's.

"We're okay." Rasping hoarsely into the phone, Pepe answered at last. "Still breathing."

Walking closer to the cliff, we found a narrow cave. A jutting ledge sheltered a long workbench hewn from an untrimmed log, a forge with a pedal to work the bellows, a basket of charcoal, a heavy anvil, a long shelf cluttered with roughly-made hammers and chisels and drills.

"The sculptor's workshop." Casey stepped back across a reef of glassy black chips on the sand, litter fallen from the chisel. "Who is the sculptor?"

He touched his lips at Pepe when Sandor called again.

"Tell him to hold the ship. Tell him we're alive and pushing inland. Tell him we've found human life, or strong evidence for it. But not a word about the face. Not till we have something Captain Vlix might believe."

We hiked inland, following a smooth-worn footpath along the riverbank. The valley widened. We came out between two rows of trees, neatly spaced, bearing bright red fruit.

"¡Cerezas!" Pepe cried. "Cherries! A cherry orchard." He picked a handful and shared them, tart, sweet, hard to believe. We came to an apple orchard, to rows of peach and pear trees, all laden with unripe fruit. We found a garden farther on, watered by a narrow ditch that diverted water from the river. Tomato vines, yams, squash, beans, tall green corn.

Casey caught his breath and stopped. I stared past him at a man—a man who might have been Sandor's double—who came striding up the path to meet us.

"Sandor?" His eager voice was almost Sandor's, though the accent made it strange. "Sandor?"

We waited, hardly breathing, while he came on to us. The image of Sandor, bronzed dark from the sun, he had the same trim frame, the same sleek brown fur crowning his head, the same pixie face and golden eyes. He stopped to scan us with evident disappointment, and pointed suddenly when he saw Pepe's radio.

Pepe let him have it. Eagerly, hands shaking, he made a call. The other Sandor answered with a quick and breathless voice. Their excited words meant nothing to me, no more than their silent communion after they fell silent, but I could read the flow of feeling on the stranger's weathered face. Wonder, fear, hope, tears of joy.

At last the Sandor on the ship had a moment for us.

"You've found my brother. Call him Corath if you need a name. Captain Vlix is ready for a jump toward the Rim. She is slow to believe what you're saying, with her ship at risk but Rokehut is demanding a chance for confirmation and I must see my brother. She's letting me come down...."

Corath beckoned. We followed him down the path till we could see the distant lake and a ruined building on a hill. Once it must have been impressive, but the stone walls were roofless now, windows and doorways black and gaping. He stopped us at his very simple residence, a thatched roof over a bare wooden floor with a small stone-walled enclosure at the rear. Waiting for Sandor, we sat at a table under the thatch. He poured cherry wine for us from a black ceramic jug and stood waiting, staring away at the sky.

Sandor landed his silvery flight pod on the grass in front of the dwelling. Corath ran to meet him. They stopped to gaze at each other, to touch each other, to grip each other's hands. They hugged and stepped apart and stood a long time face to face without a word I could hear, laughing and crying, hugging again, until at last Sandor rubbed his wet eyes and turned to us.

"I saw—saw the head." Breathing hard, he stopped to clear his throat and peer again into Corath's face as if to verify that he was real. "It was meant to be my own, though at first I thought it was his. He has been here almost two hundred years, marooned by the pathogen. With no way to search for me, he says, except inside the mountain."

A spasm of coughing bent him over. Corath held his arm till he drew himself upright and turned soberly back to us.

"We were coughing," Pepe said. "Sneezing. Wheezing. We thought we had the killer pathogen."

"Something kin to it, my brother says. But benign. He says it saved your lives."

We had to hold our questions. They forgot us, standing together a long time in silence before they laughed and embraced again. Sandor wiped at his tears at last and turned back to us.

"The pathogen got here two hundred years ago. Corath knows no more than we do about its origin or history. It caught him here on the island, at work on the same sort of nanorob research I once hoped to undertake. He was testing immunities and looking for quantum effects that might extend the contact range. The range effect is still not fully tested, but his new nanorob did make him immune. Too late to save the rest of the planet, it did wipe the pathogen off the island...."

Captain Vlix was still a stubborn skeptic, terrified of contamination. She refused to let Sandor bring his brother aboard, or even to come back himself. Yet, with Rokehut and some of the other passengers still at odds over a new destination, she let the second officer bring a little group of desperate volunteers down to see the live island for themselves.

They came off the pod jittery and pale. Fits of coughing and sneezing turned them whiter still, until Corath and his news of their new immunity brought their color back. To make his own survival sure, the officer drew a drop of Corath's blood and scratched it into his arm with a needle. Still breathing, but not yet entirely certain, he wanted to see the research station.

Corath took us to tour the ruin on the hill. The pathogen had destroyed wood and plastic, leaving only bare stone and naked steel. A quake had toppled one roofless wall, but the isolation chamber was still intact. An enormous windowless concrete box, it had heavy steel doors with an air lock between them.

Black with rust, the doors yawned open now, darkness beyond them. He struck fire with flint, steel, and tinder, lit a torch, led us inside. The chamber was empty, except for the clutter of abandoned equipment on the workbenches and a thick carpet of harmless gray dust on the floor.

We found nothing to reveal the structure of his new nanorob, nothing to explain how its wind-borne spores had set us to sneezing and made us safe. Corath answered with only a noncommittal shrug when Pepe dared to ask if the infection had made us immortal.

"At least the dust hasn't killed us," Casey said. "Good enough for me."

The officer went back to the ship with a bottle of Corath's healing blood. Captain Vlix agreed to hold the ship in orbit. Rokehut brought his engineers to survey the island and stake out a settlement site on the plateau beyond the lake. Passengers came down with their luggage and crates of freight, ready now to stake their futures on the island and Corath's promise that the red dust could make fertile soil.

He decided to stay there with them.

Sandor took us with him back aboard. Convinced at last, Captain Vlix was waiting to greet us at the airlock, embracing him almost as tearfully as his brother had. When she had finally wiped her eyes and turned away, he spoke to us.

"Our job now is to fight the pathogen with Corath's nanorob. Volunteers in flight pods are setting out to carry it to all the nearest worlds. I am taking it to Lo and Tling back on Earth. Do you want to come?"

We did.

Made in the USA
Las Vegas, NV
16 October 2023

79178270R00028